THE ULTIMATE MERGER

DELANEY DIAMOND

GARDEN AVENUE PRESS

The Ultimate Merger by Delaney Diamond

Copyright © 2012, Delaney Diamond

Garden Avenue Press

Atlanta, Georgia

ISBN: 978-0-9852838-3-4 (Ebook edition)

ISBN: 978-1-940636-52-8 (Paperback edition)

To the women below, who acted as beta readers by donating their time and offering me feedback on the story. Your assistance was greatly appreciated!

Belinda Green
Brooke Oliver
Jackie Wallace
Rahab Mugwanja
Sherika Williams
Tiffany Krepps

CHAPTER 1

*S*abrina Porter stormed in and slammed the door to her windowless office. She didn't give a damn if they heard. Slapping the sheets of paper in her hand onto the desk, she blinked back tears of anger.

It's so unfair, she thought.

She had worked harder on the Japanese project than her co-worker, Devin, but *he* was the one sitting back in his chair, smiling like a Cheshire cat, hoarding the accolades from the senior analysts. *He* was the one they decided would be the lead on the merger. And why? Because she didn't play golf?

Too wired to sit down, she paced the floor with a fist jammed into her hip bone.

A soft knock shifted her attention to the door. Before she could answer, Ernestine, the assistant she shared with Devin and four other analysts, poked in her head.

"Is it safe to come in?" she asked with a timid smile.

Sabrina gave a curt nod.

"How're you holding up?"

Ernestine pushed her gold-framed glasses up on her nose and clasped her hands in front of her. She'd been working at

Global Investments, Inc. since the formation of the company fifteen years ago. Despite the difference in their ages and the fact that Sabrina was one of her supervisors, they'd become friends when the firm hired Sabrina two years ago.

"How am I holding up? You took notes in the meeting. They gave the Japan project to Devin. That fu—" She closed her eyes and took a deep breath, letting it out slowly. Then she took another deep breath and let it out slowly, too. "That *freaking* brown-noser. Apparently, you don't need any real skill or intelligence at this firm to handle a multi-million dollar merger. All you need is a penis!"

Ernestine's pale cheeks reddened to the same shade of her hair. She cleared her throat. "You might want to lower your voice. You don't want anyone to hear you, do you?"

Sabrina let her head roll back and stared up at the ceiling, knowing Ernestine was right. "No, I don't," she said in a heavy voice. She walked over to her desk chair and collapsed onto it. "It's just so unfair. I work twice as hard as Devin does—three times, even, and I produce good work. I've been here two years, Ernestine. Two years, and every time a major deal is in the works, one of the male analysts gets it. Why am I even here? Did they have to fill a quota?"

Ernestine lowered onto the chair on the opposite side of the desk. Her sympathetic gaze connected with Sabrina's. "Your work will be recognized eventually. You'll see."

"When? I thought that busting my butt would get me recognition, but it doesn't seem to matter. As far as the senior analysts are concerned, I might as well have gone to Jane Doe University and not even bother to come in to work every day. I'd get the same amount of respect."

Ernestine took a deep breath before responding. "You're going to get even more upset when I tell you what I'm about to."

Sabrina sighed. "Lay it on me."

"They're moving Devin into a bigger office. One on the same hallway as the senior analysts."

Sabrina slumped back in the chair and stared in disbelief at her co-worker. "Are you kidding me?"

"I wish I were. I was told to start coordinating the move with the building facilities manager."

"Unbelievable."

Sabrina shook her head. She worked so hard, but it all seemed for naught. Two years ago she'd finished magna cum laude with an MBA from the University of Chicago. She'd hoped to land a job in a firm where she could work her way up in her specialty—mergers and acquisitions. However, even though she consistently churned out excellent work, she never received any of the exciting projects nor received the respect granted to her male counterparts.

"Why don't we go out for a drink tonight?" Ernestine offered. "Seems like you need it. We'll go to Giovanni's and listen to music."

"You won't drink with me."

"That doesn't mean we can't go out. I'll have cranberry juice, and you can have one of those mojitos or whatever you like—on me. How's that?"

Sabrina smiled genuinely for the first time all day. Ernestine was so sweet. Having someone in her corner helped to temper her unhappiness.

Normally, she didn't drink much because growing up, she'd seen the adverse effects of drugs and alcohol on those around her, but she needed a drink tonight.

"Nah, go home to your hubby and kids," she said. "In the mood I'm in, I'll need more than a few drinks. It might be better for me to go straight home."

Ernestine rose from the chair. "You need to get out more."

"What? You're the one who rushes home every day after work. I'm surprised you even offered to go out with me."

"And you're the one who hasn't been on a date in months."

Sabrina groaned and covered her face with her hand.

"You know it's true. Why don't you let me fix you up?"

"I don't want any more hook-ups." Last time her co-worker tried to set her up had been a disaster. The date ended in an argument with the guy calling her "you modern women" in a tone that clearly indicated it was not a compliment.

"Okay, I screwed up the last time, but I do have another man in mind for you. He's more your type. You need someone with your drive and ambition and someone who appreciates it in you. Clark wasn't the right person."

"Yah think? He practically told me he wanted me barefoot and pregnant."

"Don't exaggerate."

"I'm not."

"The man I have in mind for you this time is different. He's—"

"No." Sabrina wagged her finger at Ernestine. "Just because he's black, doesn't mean he's perfect for me. You need a better screening process, and because of that, you are not allowed to set me up ever again. Comprende?"

"One more time. I promise you'll like this one. He's nice, but he's the kind of man who could handle you."

"No. I can find my own dates, thank you very much."

"Fine." Ernestine headed for the door. Before walking out, she said, "If you change your mind, let me know. The right man can help you relieve some of this work-related stress."

"If I need to relieve stress, I'll get a massage."

"It's been so long, you've forgotten how good it can be." With a saucy wiggle to her hips, Ernestine reached for the doorknob.

Sabrina shook her head. "You have your husband wrapped around your finger, don't you?"

Laughing, Ernestine said, "I'll see you later," before closing the door behind her.

Sabrina took a deep breath and swiveled in her chair to face the computer screen. She needed a man like she needed a hole in her head. Besides, if she wanted to get laid, she knew who to call. In fact...

She picked up the phone and punched in the number to her friend-with-benefits, Samuel. It had been a long time since they'd connected, but maybe she'd get lucky and he'd be free tonight.

"Hello, beautiful."

What a nice way to be greeted. "Hey, you busy tonight?"

"No. What did you have in mind?"

"Dinner and drinks at Giovanni's. My treat."

"Do I have to put out if you buy me dinner?"

She twirled the phone cord around her forefinger. "Yes."

He chuckled, and she imagined his coffee-colored eyes crinkling at the corners. "Rough day?"

Sabrina sighed. "Yeah, you could say that."

"I got you. Call me before you leave work and I'll meet you there."

"Thanks." Sabrina hung up.

Now she had something to look forward to at the end of the day.

CHAPTER 2

*R*enaldo da Silva stood and stretched in the living room of the suite he had at The Drake Hotel in downtown Chicago. He rolled his shoulders to alleviate the tension in his muscles. He might as well have been in a basement for all the attention he paid to the deluxe room with its stunning view of Lake Michigan in the distance.

Ever since he'd arrived in Illinois a few days ago, he'd been in and out of meetings and spent the rest of his time on his laptop conducting research and communicating with his staff. He'd hoped to be farther along in the deal by now, but he'd just have to be patient a little while longer.

He flexed his shoulders and grabbed the room key from the desk. He'd been in the room all day, and it was now dark outside. He needed a break. Time to get out and see a little bit of what Chicago had to offer.

Downstairs, he asked for a recommendation to a place where he could get a drink and unwind. Before long, he headed out on foot to a nearby restaurant recommended by the concierge. When he arrived at Giovanni's he could hear music playing and the weekend crowd had already started gathering.

One of the best ways to relieve stress was in the arms of a woman. Unfortunately, he'd been so busy he hadn't had time to make the acquaintance of anyone during his short stay. The energy of the patrons and the beat of rock music would have to suffice tonight.

Renaldo sat at the bar and ordered a scotch. As he nursed his drink, mentally listing everything he had to accomplish next week, a tall black woman walked in. She entered the restaurant with a straight spine and a confident walk. At first he gave her only a cursory glance. She appeared to have just left work, dressed in a plain gray business suit with a white silk blouse and very little jewelry. After she took a seat at the opposite end of the bar, his eyes strayed to her again.

With her kinky, chestnut-colored hair pulled back from her face and clipped neatly at the back of her head, he couldn't tell its true length. She didn't wear much makeup on her tawny-colored skin. Good thing, too, because she had an attractive face.

In one graceful movement, she removed her blazer and then twisted on the stool to hang it over the back of the chair, the motion causing the silk blouse to pull taut across her chest. He was a breast man, and she had two nice-looking ones. Not big, but enough to almost fill his hands. His jaw tightened at the thought as he swirled the scotch in the glass. He hoped she was alone. If so, his situation might be improving.

He enjoyed burying his face in the perfumed cleft of a woman's cleavage. What would the cleft between her breasts smell like? The thought stirred his loins awake.

As he watched her, Renaldo wondered, too, about the color of her eyes. Were they brown or black? He soon received an answer. She idly scanned the room and her gaze landed on him. White heat pooled in his stomach, causing him to halt the swirling motion of his hand.

Light brown. Stunning.

* * *

SABRINA DIDN'T THINK she could have experienced a greater shock if the force of a lightning bolt had coursed through her body. For a moment she froze, bewitched by a pair of eyes as black as midnight.

Unnerved, she dragged her eyes away, but not before she registered the man's other features: an aquiline nose, short-cut hair the same color of his eyes, and swarthy skin which suggested he might be Italian or Latin. His white shirt opened at the collar to reveal a strong throat and a sprinkling of crisp, black hair.

Even though she'd looked away, she knew he still watched. She could feel it.

"What can I get for you?" the bartender asked with a friendly smile.

She ordered a glass of red wine. When he walked away, she picked up the menu to check out the selection of appetizers, disregarding the biting intensity of the feelings that had just flowed through her. A few minutes later, she placed an order for stuffed mushrooms and had a glass of wine in her hand.

Glancing around the bar, careful not to look straight ahead again, she regretted telling Ernestine not to come. They always had fun when they hung out together. Well, she'd have the next best thing soon enough. She'd left Samuel a voice mail before she left work, so he should be here soon.

Unable to resist, she let her eyes drift back across the bar. A pretty brunette had joined the man, and he bent his head to her as they talked. Sabrina stared down into the maroon liquid in her glass. She was meeting Samuel, and she didn't have dibs on the stranger, but a feeling of disappointment stole over her.

Between the problems at work and her overactive imagination about a complete stranger, she was on her way to winning the award for Doom and Gloom. During moments like these, the doubts started creeping in, and she needed a distraction from the empty void she feared her life had become.

"Nice band," she said to the bartender as he set a newly replenished bowl of nuts nearby. "I don't think I've ever seen them play here before."

"They're new. This is only their second night." He walked away to take another patron's order.

She drummed her fingers against the top of the bar and did what she shouldn't—compared her life to Ernestine's. At forty, Ernestine was fourteen years older than Sabrina, and she had a husband and a family waiting for her. When she walked through the door, their eyes would light up and they'd be happy to see her. Maybe her son and daughter would even rush into her arms the minute she crossed the threshold.

Sabrina's fingers slowed to a stop, and she swallowed hard to shut out the painful memories of growing up on the South Side of Chicago. The emotional scars kept her focused on the prize of success, but there were times when she wanted...She lifted the glass to her lips and took a sip of the fruity wine, shutting her eyes and welcoming the darkness for several seconds.

She wanted to be welcomed home. She wanted someone to miss her, need her. But the truth was, she feared taking the leap. She didn't want her plans derailed, and getting involved with a man who didn't understand her focus and drive could do that.

As a child, she'd managed to survive when her mother would disappear for days at a time, leaving her and her younger cousin in the apartment alone to fend for themselves. She knew what it was like to live on nothing but stale bread and ketchup or whatever she could beg for from the neighbors. Inconceivable to most people, but that was the world she'd known, and she could never go back to it.

The memories made her bust her butt every single day to succeed in the male-dominated world of the career she'd chosen

—Plan A. She didn't even have a Plan B because failure wasn't an option.

Again she cast what she hoped was a surreptitious glance over to the other side. He and the brunette were no longer there.

Sabrina's phone vibrated, and she retrieved it from her purse. Samuel had texted her. Something had come up and he had to cancel. She sighed heavily. She couldn't win for losing today. What a great way to coast into the weekend.

"Excuse me." A low, accented, very male voice spoke beside her. Sabrina looked up, and up into the dark depths of a pair of eyes set in a face even more striking up close. A knot formed deep in her belly. He held a drink in one hand. "My name is Renaldo da Silva. Do you mind if I join you?"

CHAPTER 3

a quiver of awareness inched down Sabrina's spine. Despite the half smile on his lips and the casual way he'd tucked one hand into his trouser pocket, she knew without a doubt that this man didn't do casual. He was big, easily six-foot-five, or very near it. Power emanated from him.

She motioned toward the empty stool. "It's all yours."

He lowered himself beside her. "And your name is…?" he prompted.

Here we go. "This isn't a good time, okay?"

"All I did was ask your name." Sabrina remained silent. "Don't tell me I misread the signal I received from across the bar."

"I'm afraid you did. I never sent you a signal."

"So you expect me to believe you're not interested at all?"

She gave him a saccharine smile. "I suppose you're used to women throwing themselves at your feet. Is that it?"

"Yes, that's normally how it happens."

He smiled, and her stomach clenched in reaction. In addition to having a killer smile and being fine as hell, he also had a sense of humor. The man was definitely dangerous.

Sabrina tried to relax, but she remained acutely aware of him, which made it impossible to relax. She couldn't remember the last time she'd been this attracted to a man at the first encounter—if ever.

He rested his forearm on the edge of the bar and turned toward her, giving her his full attention. "You are from Chicago?"

She tried to decipher where he could be from by his accent. "Yes, I am. And you?"

"Brazil. I'm here on business. What did you say your name was again?"

"Nice try. I didn't."

"I love a challenge. It's a turn on."

Sabrina took a steadying breath. How in the world could any woman fight against this type of persistence? "So that means you're not going to leave me alone to enjoy my glass of wine? By myself."

"Yes, that's what it means."

Before responding, she hesitated, pretending to consider whether or not she should answer. "Sabrina."

"Was that so hard?"

He'd probably never had to work this hard to get a woman's name before. "No." She pursed her lips and decided to make conversation. "How long will you be here on business?"

"About three weeks." His face remained unreadable as he studied her. "This is my first visit to Chicago."

"Oh. Well, you'll enjoy it here. There's plenty to do and see."

"So I've been told." He waited a heartbeat and then added, "Maybe you could show me around?" His forthrightness didn't surprise her. He didn't strike her as the kind of man who beat around the bush.

Sabrina laughed. "No, I don't think so."

"Why not?"

She eyed him with suspicion lacing her gaze. "You'd be better off with a tour company."

"I'd rather have personalized service."

Her heart fluttered, but she remained cool. "There are plenty of reputable companies offering sightseeing tours," she pointed out. "You can see the city by bus, or another popular type of tour is the architectural river tour. It takes you down the Chicago River. Trust me, you'll be in good hands."

His lids lowered so that his dark eyes became half-hidden. "I'd rather be in your hands."

Heat spread across her breasts, and Sabrina could feel her nipples hardening beneath her lacy bra. She took a huge swallow of wine. "I bet you say that to all the girls." He laughed, the rich sound bouncing between them and startling her stomach into a quiver that had her taking a calming breath. "I'm sorry, I can't help you. I don't know you from Adam."

His thick black brows came together. "Adam? Who is this Adam?"

"It's an expression." She smiled. "It basically means I don't know you."

"You have a lovely smile. I believe this time it was real." He leaned closer, and the enticing mélange of his cologne—dark spices and a zesty citrus scent—drifted up into her nostrils. "What would you like to know about me?"

He held her gaze and made her feel like the only person in the entire establishment.

"Okay," she said, pressing against the back of the chair, adding a few inches of space between them to clear her head. "For starters, what kind of business are you in?"

Before he could answer, the bartender set her order on the bar with a small plate and silverware. She signaled toward the dish, making Renaldo a silent offer. He shook his head.

"Real estate," he replied. "Renovations mostly, although I'd like to eventually expand into construction. For now, I concentrate on purchasing commercial properties like hotels and office buildings, gut them, modernize them, and then turn around and sell them for a profit. I'm in Chicago trying to close on a hotel." He lifted an eyebrow. "What else?"

Sabrina cocked her head to one side. "You really think all you have to do is give me a few facts about yourself and then I'll…what exactly?"

His eyes filled with amusement. "Show me around your beautiful city. Nothing more."

"And that's all you want?"

He paused in the act of lifting the crystal glass of amber spirit to his lips. When he answered, his voice had lowered another octave. "It is too early in our acquaintance to tell you what I really want."

CHAPTER 4

*S*he knew she shouldn't ask, but she chose to throw caution to the wind. "And what is it that you really want?"

He didn't hesitate. "You."

His answer left her breathless. Their gazes clashed. "I see you're not shy about speaking your mind."

"Would you expect anything less?" A sexy smile hovered around his mouth.

"No, I guess I wouldn't."

"That's what I thought."

Sabrina allowed her forefinger to slide around the circumference of the rim of her glass. "What happened to the brunette?"

"She wasn't my type."

"And I am?" Her fingertip halted its movement. "What exactly is your type, may I ask?"

"I like women who are confident and independent. You seem to be both."

"Somehow I envisioned men from Brazil as being more...I don't know...traditional in their views."

"I have to admit, I can be old-fashioned in some ways. I never let a woman pay when we're dating."

Sabrina lifted a brow in surprise. "Never?"

"Never. It's my responsibility. I open doors, and when we're walking down the street, I insist the woman I'm with walks on the inside, away from the traffic."

Sabrina laughed as she spooned two mushrooms onto her plate. "You *are* old school. You don't see that much nowadays. But what you said doesn't fit with your desire for an independent woman." In her experience, men always said they wanted an independent woman, but when they found her, they couldn't handle it.

"Actually, it does. You see, I grew up in a traditional household. My father was the head of the house, and my mother never worked. He took care of her, doted on her, and she wanted for nothing. When he passed away, she couldn't even balance a check book. We lost our business and struggled for several years." Regret—or maybe sadness—entered his eyes for a moment. "I wish they were both alive to see how well my sisters and I are doing now."

Sabrina nodded her head in understanding. "I know the feeling," she murmured.

She stared down at the maroon liquid in her glass. She would do anything to have her mother back, to show her how much she had achieved, despite the rough start to life. The pain and guilt never seemed to go away. She never stopped wondering if she could have done something different and saved her mother.

* * *

THEY FELL INTO AN EASY CONVERSATION. She forgot all about her previous plans and spent the next forty minutes listening to Renaldo talk mostly about his business and the stress to close the deal he was working on. He was successful, but not quite where he wanted to be. One of his goals was to expand into the U.S. market. In between the business talk, they flirted and bantered back and forth, and he educated her on the culture of his country.

"I'm doing all the talking," Renaldo said. "What do you do for a living?"

"I'm a financial analyst for a firm named Global Investments. My focus is mergers and acquisitions."

"Really? Maybe I can steal you away from your firm. I could use a knowledgeable analyst on my team, and you're based here in Chicago, where I hope to begin my expansion into the U.S."

"If I didn't think you were kidding, I'd take you up on the offer," Sabrina said dryly.

Renaldo frowned. "You're not happy?"

"Let's just say things could be better. I'm out tonight to drown my sorrows in red wine and forget my problems at work." She pushed a lukewarm mushroom around on her plate with the fork. "I sound bitter, don't I?"

What was she thinking? Sitting here with an attractive man paying her attention, and all she could do was complain about her job. She should be thinking about engaging in more pleasurable activities with him, because right now the alternative— going home to an empty apartment and Netflix—did not appeal at all.

"If you're unhappy, why don't you leave?"

"Yeah, I'll just walk out of there and find another job just like that." Sabrina snapped her fingers. "I'll suffer through it."

"Like you're doing now?" he asked pointedly. "Spending a Friday night alone at a bar?"

His questions hit home in a way she didn't like. "I'm not really alone, though, am I?" She shrugged. "I wanted to unwind before going home. It's been a long week and an even longer day. Actually, I had plans, but my friend cancelled at the last minute."

"And this friend…was it a man?"

She eyed him from the corner of her eye, surprised he'd deduced that so easily. "Yes."

"Foolish man," Renaldo said in a low tone.

"He's usually dependable. I'm sure he has a good reason why he couldn't make it."

"I'm sure," Renaldo said, sounding unconvinced. "Fortunately, he's not here, but I am."

Sabrina ran her tongue along the inside of her upper lip. "What does that mean?" she asked.

"It means I'd like to take his place."

CHAPTER 5

*H*e watched the play of emotions across her face.

"Excuse me?" she said.

Although she feigned ignorance of his intentions, he didn't believe it for one minute. If they offered degrees in reading women's body language, he'd have a Ph.D. There was no misunderstanding the flirtatious smiles or sidelong glances as they'd conversed. If her body burned for his as much as his burned for her, they could both get the release they craved.

"Are we going to pretend we don't want the same thing?"

She opened her mouth to speak, but refrained from doing so. She swallowed and turned her attention back to her dish. It had to be cold and unappetizing by now, but she placed another mushroom into her pretty mouth in an obvious effort to keep herself busy.

His mind conjured an image of her putting him in her mouth. The vivid thought caused his muscles to seize, and for a moment he couldn't move. When he regained his motor skills, he knew there could only be one outcome. He desperately wanted this woman. Tonight.

"I've spent the last forty-five minutes thinking about what I would have to say to make you feel comfortable enough to leave here with me," he said.

His eyes lowered to the fast-beating pulse at the vee of her blouse. His own breathing became irregular, as if he'd exerted himself in some form of physical exercise.

"Nothing you say will convince me to leave with you," she said in a husky undertone. She drained the last of her second glass of wine and reached for her purse.

"What are you doing?"

"I'm leaving."

"Why?"

"Why?" She laughed, and it sounded uneasy. "Because something's wrong with me. I should be offended, or disgusted, or something. But instead—" Her light brown eyes scanned his face, and then they darted away again. She got down off the stool.

He stood, too. "Instead what?" he prompted.

She shook her head vigorously and grabbed the blazer from the back of the chair. Automatically, he helped her into it. Once it was on, she clutched the open edges like a safety jacket.

"Instead what?" he whispered in her ear. She smelled good. Not the scent of perfume or lotion. It was just the scent of a woman. Her natural, sweet fragrance.

"Instead…" Color blossomed in her cheeks. "Instead…I'm considering it."

The noise from the bar disappeared; the sound of silverware hitting plates disappeared. The chatter and laughter of patrons became nonexistent. All his senses became attuned to the woman standing before him.

"What do you need?" he asked, because he didn't know what else to do. He was accustomed to negotiations, but right now, a compromise was the furthest thing from his mind. He wanted her to come with him, and he didn't care what he had to do or give up to make it happen. He wanted her to feel comfortable enough to leave a crowded establishment and go back to his room and let him have his way with her. "My identification, a fingerprint, a blood sample? Whatever you want, I will give it."

* * *

HIS PERSISTENCE TURNED HER ON. She liked persistence in a man —a man who knew what he wanted and pursued until he captured it.

Perhaps it was the wine, or the loneliness she felt, or the disappointment about her job. Perhaps it was a combination of all those things. Whatever it was, it prompted Sabrina to say, "That won't be necessary."

A weight seemed to have been lifted. The tension left over from the stressful day at work oozed from her shoulders. Now that she'd made the decision, she actually felt better.

She swallowed down the last remnants of her unease. "Where are you staying?"

She saw the flash of hunger in his eyes, and a spark of desire emerged in her belly.

"The Drake."

She nodded and reached inside her purse to cover the tab.

"Allow me." He pulled out his wallet.

"That won't be—"

"I insist."

He called over the bartender and handed him some bills. He didn't bother waiting for his change, giving more than enough to cover both checks and leave a generous tip. He moved quickly, as if he didn't want to give her the opportunity to change her mind.

Not that she would. She figured she probably should, but what she knew to do and what she did were two separate things. What she knew to do was turn around, walk away, and embrace her empty life. Like always.

To hell with it.

She placed her hand in his.

She didn't want to be alone tonight, so she followed him out into the night.

CHAPTER 6

The door of the suite clicked shut.

"Would you like a drink?" Renaldo asked behind her.

"No." Sabrina's heart was beating so fast she almost couldn't speak.

He came closer in the dark, so close the heat from his body warmed her back. The drapes opened to the night outside, and she could see the lights from the other buildings. The large room was filled with shadowy furnishings—lamps, a desk, sofas, tables. A door to the left led into what she assumed was the bedroom.

He rested his hands on her shoulders. "Relax."

"Maybe this was a bad idea." The fierce beating of her heart indicated she might be in over her head.

He massaged the knot at the top of her spine. "You still do not trust me. You're second-guessing yourself." The whispered words in her ear made her skin come alive with tiny pinpricks of heat.

"And you're not? I could be a thief or a murderer."

The circular motion of his thumbs continued to caress

through her clothes, turning her limbs to liquid so that her purse slid from her shoulder to the carpet.

His arms folded around her and he pulled her tighter to his body. "I'll take my chances."

His mouth drifted up the side of her neck, delivering little kisses that made her shiver and ache. The soft pressure of his mouth inflamed her skin, and she almost melted into a puddle at his feet.

"From the minute I saw you," he said, his voice gruff, "I knew."

"How did you know?" she asked in a husky whisper.

He turned her in his arms and gently tugged the tail of her blouse from the waistband of her skirt as he gazed into her eyes. "The same way you did."

He took his time undoing her top, the silence troubled by the sound of her uneven breathing. When he'd released each button, he kissed the crests of her breasts and pressed his face to her cleavage, inhaling deeply.

His mouth moved to her neck, and he whispered in a rasping voice, "This is no mistake."

Squeezing her breasts together, his thick thumbs teased her nipples with firm, insistent strokes through the black lace until she gasped and arched into his hands.

No, this was no mistake. Such delicious pleasure could not be wrong.

With deft fingers, he undid her skirt, and it fell quietly onto the carpet. Her blouse followed suit. He caressed the newly exposed skin of her hips in a pair of lace panties, warming the flesh and making her ache.

The way she responded seemed to start a fire in him. He pulled her into the power of his body and lowered his head to take her mouth in a passionately bruising kiss. Prying her lips apart with his tongue, he stole her breath and demanded more in a hungry invasion that left her wanting more.

One hand at the back of her head fumbled with the clip until he'd loosened it to run his fingers through the short, spiral strands of her hair. His right hand palmed her buttocks and forced her to acknowledge his hard erection.

Sabrina wrapped her arms around the wide trunk of his body, feeling his heart pound against her chest. When he lifted his head, she looked up at him in amazement.

"I think I'm wearing too many clothes," he said.

"We both are."

They stripped in the near-darkness and tossed their clothing and shoes aside, unconcerned about where each item landed.

Renaldo slipped on a condom and then bent his head to her breasts, sucking her nipples and gently biting them until she cried out, digging her short nails into his broad shoulders. He smoothed his hand down her buttocks and between her thighs, letting his fingers slide through the slickness to test her readiness.

"Turn around." He took her by the shoulders and twisted her to face away from him. Her heart raced, unsure of what to expect next.

"Bend over," he said, his voice a dark rumble.

"Wh-what?" Sabrina cast a glance of alarm over her shoulder at him.

He pressed his lips to her ear. "Relax. Trust me. You're going to love it. Place your hands on the floor."

One muscular arm curved around her waist, and he grasped the back of her neck. Easing her forward, he forced her to bend at the hip. His foot shoved her feet apart, spreading her legs wider for him. Her breath stuttered in her chest and her body trembled in the vulnerable position in which he'd placed her. With her hips elevated against his groin, he found the wet entrance to her body and pushed in all the way—uttering a low groan—lodging deep inside of her.

Sabrina's eyes squeezed shut as she savored the sensation of his deep penetration. He eased out slowly and then shoved back in again.

"*Oh,*" she moaned, her legs shaking as pleasure soared through her, her palms pressing down onto the floor to help maintain her balance.

Holding her in place, he pulled back and plunged downward repeatedly, skin slapping against skin with each thrust.

He muttered in Portuguese. She had no idea what he said, but it didn't matter. His beautiful voice made her sex convulse while he drove into her, stirring the flames of passion into a frenzied flash-fire that burned hotter than she'd ever experienced.

This was exactly what she needed. This intensity. This release.

Inside, she tightened, nearing an internal explosion. A sob fled her lips. Pressure mounted, and his continued whispers in his own language urged her closer to the edge.

Then she lost control.

Waves of sensation crashed over her. She cried out, the room spinning as her body convulsed. He held her upright against him, his fingers pressing into the flesh of her hips.

Then he lost control.

She heard the broken groan when he could no longer hold back.

He pushed in with more urgency, tightening his grip on her. He pumped faster, grunting, and then, just when she thought she couldn't take any more, he began to grind his hips against her. The coarse hair of his genitals chafed the sensitive skin of her buttocks as he erupted.

Weakened, Sabrina collapsed to her knees, and he came down behind her. They remained in that position for a while with a film of sweat on their skin, their breaths coming short and hard. His naked flesh warmed hers, and his chest hairs tickled her back.

He rose to his feet, lifted her into his arms, and carried her to his bed.

Later, lying comfortably beneath the sheets, Sabrina turned her face into his neck and inhaled deeply of his manly scent. Her fingers caressed the silken threads of hair on his head. She was so comfortable she never wanted to leave the circle of his arms.

As quickly as the thought came, it disappeared again, pushed away by common sense. She couldn't let good sex cloud her thinking, and what she'd just experienced was better than good. It was amazing.

"Feeling better now?" Renaldo asked, his breath brushing her forehead. His fingertips stroked down her spine, leaving tiny shivers in their wake.

"Mhmm." Sabrina slid her leg along the length of his calf. "I'm not tense anymore."

After a little chuckle, he kissed her forehead. "Glad to hear it."

Drifting into sleep, Sabrina wondered what the hell she'd gotten herself into.

CHAPTER 7

S abrina hadn't expected to meet the man of her dreams a month ago, but life had a way of throwing curve balls. Never in her wildest dreams as a young girl growing up on the mean streets of Englewood—on the South Side of Chicago—had she ever thought she'd be lying in a king bed in a posh suite at The Drake Hotel.

The enormous room was the size of a small apartment, with a separate living room, dining room, and bedroom. Decorated in warm colors, fine linens, and heavy drapes, it had become her home away from home. Nowadays, she spent more time here than she did in her own apartment.

Because of him.

She'd fallen hopelessly in love in such a short time, and it scared her. She dreaded the end of the relationship, but the end loomed near. Once he concluded the deal he'd been working on, Renaldo would return to his country. Lucky for her, he'd hit a few snags and the real estate closing had been delayed.

Sabrina rolled over and stared at her lover's back as he stood looking out one of the windows at the breathtaking view of Lake Michigan. With one arm braced on the window frame, he spoke in a low tone into the phone so as not to disturb her, not knowing she was still awake. Her eyes drifted over his bare back and the solid beams of his long legs in a pair of black boxer briefs that clung to his firm buttocks.

Renaldo da Silva was every woman's dream. Muscles covered each inch of tanned flesh, and every night they spent together she received such pleasure that she closed her eyes momentarily as warm sensations filled her.

When she lifted her lids, she saw he'd turned toward her. His onyx-colored eyes swept over the imprint of her body beneath the covers. Heat swelled within her, and she welcomed his attention, even though they'd already made love this morning.

He said something into the mouthpiece of the phone. Then she heard him say, *"Adeus,"* never taking his eyes from her, before he hung up and placed the phone on a table against the wall.

She smiled. "Are you coming back to bed now?"

One corner of his mouth slanted upward. "You were not satisfied earlier? I'm not doing my job very well." He walked with confidence toward the bed, and Sabrina dragged the sheet down her skin to unveil her body and invite him onto the mattress with her.

He growled low in his throat, eyes darkening as his gaze swept her nakedness. The creep of moisture between her thighs readied her for him. She wanted him in the worst way.

"I guess you'll have to work harder," she whispered breathlessly.

He lowered onto the bed and slipped his hand between her open legs. He tenderly kissed the corner of her mouth while his fingers stroked with skill.

"Sim," he whispered. He lifted his head and looked down at her beneath half-lowered lids. "I will work very, very hard this time, *meu amor.*"

With a wicked grin, he covered her body and went to work.

* * *

Two days later, Sabrina arrived at her job with a smile on her face, all because she'd spent another satisfying night with Renaldo—or Renny, as she teasingly called him. She was enjoying this little affair too much. She should thank her employer for getting on her nerves or she would never have gone out that Friday night, and then she never would have met Renaldo.

When she considered the men she'd been involved with in the past, no one else compared. She'd dropped her friend-with-benefits, Samuel. All because Renaldo had become absolutely addictive.

They had so much in common. They were both driven, with a strong work ethic. Because of that, he treated her as an equal and didn't try to put her in a box. Several times he'd bounced ideas off of her and asked her opinion about aspects of the hotel purchase. She'd been flattered he valued her opinion so much and wished she could garner the same respect at her place of employment.

On the weekends, she took him around the city. At one of her favorite pizza joints, they ate authentic Chicago-style pizza, a deep-dish pie filled with cheese, chunky tomato sauce, and meat and vegetable toppings. One weekend she joined him on a bus tour of the city. She'd learned some things herself as she listened to the guide. They also set sail on a one-hour architectural cruise and listened as the young woman explained how the city bounced back from the Great Fire of 1871 to become a show piece of modern American architecture.

One of her favorite things was learning his language. She knew how to count to twenty in Portuguese now, and he'd gotten into the habit of teaching her two new expressions every day.

Bom dia. Good morning.

Boa tarde. Good afternoon.

De onde você é? Where are you from?

Desculpe. I'm sorry.

And her favorite words: *Até amanhã.* See you tomorrow.

Sabrina entered the tall, glass-covered building on Michigan Avenue and rode the elevator up to the floor where she worked. On the way to her office, Ernestine's voice stopped her in her tracks.

"Sabrina, you have a visitor."

The look in the other woman's eyes made her uneasy. Her fingers curled tighter around the covered cup of coffee in her hand, and she hitched her leather business bag higher on her shoulder. She started to lose the buzz from her morning high.

"Who is it?"

"She didn't give her name, but she said she's your cousin...?" The feeling of dread increased exponentially. Ernestine lifted one brow higher, her tone and expression suggesting either she doubted they were family, or she didn't comprehend how they could be. "She's in the restroom right now."

Taking a deep breath, Sabrina forced what she hoped looked like a genuine smile onto her face. "When she comes out, please send her back to my office."

Ernestine nodded and Sabrina stepped quickly down the hall, not bothering to pause and say "Good morning" to her officemates like she usually did. She couldn't, because her mind reeled at the thought that Jewel was here, at her workplace.

It had to be Jewel, because she was the only family Sabrina kept in contact with in Chicago. She'd walked away from the old neighborhood years ago—the crime, the filth, the drugs, the dysfunction. She wanted no part of the old life to connect with her career.

But Jewel was here.

CHAPTER 8

Oh my God.

Sabrina's mouth fell open as she stared at her cousin's bedraggled appearance from behind her desk.

Her cousin's eyes filled with embarrassment. "Hi, Brina."

Jewel Porter looked like she'd been dragged through a sewer once, and dragged through it again for good measure. Her skin, the same buttery color as Sabrina's, was covered in dirt and had an unhealthy pallor to it. Her long hair was disheveled and clumped together in several places. And the smell…

"Jewel," she whispered, her heart hurting. She raced around the desk.

"No." Jewel stepped back, lowered her eyes and shook her head. "I don't want to get you dirty. I-I just…" Her face crumbled.

"What happened to you?" This was the worst she'd ever seen her.

Three months had passed since they last saw each other, and Sabrina had begun to wonder if her cousin had died. She'd never stayed away this long before. She hadn't even called once the entire time. Sabrina called the police and checked at hospitals, each time sagging with relief when no one fitting her cousin's description was in either location.

Her gaunt appearance terrified Sabrina. When had she last eaten? Other than drugs, what else was she putting into her body?

Jewel kept her eyes trained on the floor. "I'm sorry, Brina. I need your help. I don't know where else to go. I tried to reach you at home, but…but you were never there. I didn't know how else to get in touch with you."

Sabrina had been having a good time, spending every possible moment with Renaldo, when her cousin had needed her. The weight of guilt came down on her conscience.

"I'm here for you. You know that."

Jewel covered her face and cried. She barely made a sound, which made it even more heart-wrenching. Sabrina gripped her cousin's arms. She was so stick-thin that Sabrina's fingers touched her thumb.

"Look at me. Look at me, Jewel." Her voice shook, because she was scared. She knew what could happen. They'd been raised together and were practically sisters. They'd both lost their mothers to drugs. She couldn't lose Jewel, too. She wouldn't let it happen.

Jewel's empty, tear-filled eyes finally lifted.

"We'll beat this, okay? We'll do it together. You and me, just like always."

Jewel nodded like a child, looking needy and trusting.

Sabrina rushed around her desk and grabbed her bag. She picked up the phone and told Ernestine she had a family emergency and was leaving for the day.

"Come on," she said, pulling Jewel behind her. First, she had to get her cousin cleaned up and give her clothes to wear. Then they'd go to a doctor.

She didn't even want to know what Jewel had been up to. She already knew what happened when women ran out of money because she'd seen her mother do it. They used their bodies as currency.

* * *

RENALDO STARED at his phone on the desk in his suite. He rubbed his fingers across his jaw. He tried not to succumb to the need to call Sabrina again. He'd already texted and called her this morning. It was now mid-afternoon and he still hadn't heard from her. Very unusual.

He didn't like not having answers. He picked up the phone and examined it, checking his list of texts to make sure he hadn't missed any. No missed voicemails, either.

Where was she?

Should he be worried? Was she busy today? Or was she blowing him off?

* * *

THURSDAY MORNING, Renaldo sat in the real estate closing signing documents. The deal was done, yet he had unfinished business.

He hadn't seen Sabrina in three days, the longest period since they'd started their affair. A short text from her didn't explain much except that she was very busy with a family issue. Her explanation surprised him because he could count on one hand the number of times she'd provided any information about her family. When he offered to help, she'd turned him down, stating she could take care of it on her own.

Whatever "it" was took up a lot of her time. Not only had she cut off contact with him, but when he showed up at her job unannounced, he discovered she'd taken leave from work. What was going on that caused someone like her to leave work?

With a flight booked to leave for Brazil tomorrow, he

wanted to see her before he left. Maybe he was being selfish, but he needed to see her. Needed. Not wanted. Needed. She'd become as important to him as breathing.

"Last one," the attorney said, pushing another piece of paper at him to sign.

He scribbled his signature in blue ink and then rose from the chair.

"Congratulations."

Renaldo didn't return the man's smile. "Let's wrap this up," he said, casting an impatient glance at his watch.

"Certainly, sir. I'll put together your packet of documents. As a reminder, if we find any errors later, you're required to…"

Renaldo tuned out the attorney. All he could think about was Sabrina. He didn't want to leave without saying a proper goodbye. And he wanted to talk to her about their relationship. He'd be back and forth to the United States now, and he intended to continue seeing her. Did she want to continue seeing him?

CHAPTER 9

*S*abrina stepped out of the shower and rubbed lotion all over her skin. She sprayed on a light fragrance and finger-combed her hair, loosening the curls and forcing them into a position that framed her face.

Now she had Jewel settled in a treatment facility, she felt more at ease and planned to return to work on Monday.

She donned her green silk robe and stepped out of the bathroom into the master bedroom of her two-bedroom apartment. She didn't need the two bedrooms, but she kept them because of Jewel. Her cousin had come and gone out of her life over the years. Whenever Jewel cleaned up, she always stayed with Sabrina.

When they were younger, safety and cleanliness were a luxury they couldn't afford. As two parentless teens, they'd struggled to make ends meet.

Jewel's downward slide started slowly. First, underage drinking. Then weed. Then the dreaded crack. During Sabrina's freshman year in college, Jewel, two years younger than she, had fallen prey to the same drug that had taken the life of Sabrina's mother.

Only in recent years had Sabrina herself started drinking. Drugs had never been an option after seeing how it destroyed her family and the people around her. Jewel had always been a daredevil and rebellious. Her rebellious spirit had been her downfall.

Sabrina had no intention of ever turning her back on her, though. As far as she was concerned, Jewel was her sister, just like their mothers had been sisters. She would always look out for her and make sure she was safe. Maybe this stint in rehab would work. It had to. Her cousin's appearance had scared her so much this time, she worried Jewel would end up dead.

She walked into the living room with a black dress in hand, pulled the ironing board from the closet, and set it up. Now she had to talk to Renaldo. She'd avoided him long enough. He was leaving the country tomorrow, and she couldn't let him leave without seeing him one more time.

She loved him, and she wanted to say a proper goodbye. At this point, she didn't even know if he wanted to see her, but she had to try.

A knock sounded on the door. She wasn't expecting anyone. She set the dress on the ironing board.

"Who is it?"

No answer, but the knock came again, louder this time, sounding like a sledgehammer.

She stood in the hallway for a moment, and then she tiptoed to the door and peered through the peep hole.

Renaldo! Her heart skipped a beat.

She undid the safety latch and swung open the door. "Renny!" The smile on her face died a quick death when he stared back at her with an angry scowl.

"Where have you been?"

Her charming Brazilian looked like he wanted to wring her neck.

* * *

RENALDO PUSHED his way into the apartment.

"I told you, I had a family emergency."

"A family emergency?" he repeated. He took a look at the ironing board and the little black dress draped across it and pressed his lips together in a thin line. His head rotated back to her in her silk robe, smelling freshly showered and wearing the scent of pink lilies he loved so much. "Looks to me like you have plans tonight."

"No," she said, shaking her head emphatically. "It's not what you think. I planned to call you, to see if I could come see you."

"Was that before or after your date?" Jealousy ate at him, grinding in his gut.

"I don't have a date," Sabrina said. "How could you think that?"

"What am I to think?" Renaldo ground out. "I have not heard anything from you in days, and when I did, it was a cryptic message that didn't tell me much. Yet, I show up here, and you look like you're getting ready to go out for the night. But I'm supposed to believe you planned to call me?"

"I was. I know you're leaving tomorrow."

She put her hand up to massage the back of her neck, and the movement made Renaldo take notice of her appearance. Her eyes held a tiredness in them, and he wondered if she'd been having difficulty sleeping. He certainly had. At night, he kept reaching for her, and when his arms came up empty, he woke up and couldn't get back to sleep.

"What's wrong?" he asked.

"Nothing."

He walked toward her. "What is this family emergency you had?"

"There's nothing you can do." She looked like someone who

had the weight of the world on her shoulders and didn't know how to ditch it.

"Are you in some kind of trouble? Is it your job?"

"No. I don't want to talk about it. It's personal, and I'll get over it. You can't help me, and you'll be gone tomorrow anyway." She passed him on her way to the ironing board. "I'll get dressed and we can—"

Renaldo took her by the arm and forced her around to face him. He tilted her chin up toward him, searching her face. "Tell me what's wrong. We're not leaving until you do."

* * *

Sabrina twisted out of his grasp. She'd taken great pains to keep her past a secret. What was she supposed to tell him? That she was one of the lucky ones, having grown up in a community known to be a haven for crime, where drug dealers ruled the streets and violence kept children indoors?

"Sabrina…?"

His probing gaze held her captive. She wanted so badly to tell him everything and unburden her soul. But it was easier to keep her secrets to herself and wear the mask of independence and strength, while wondering the entire time if she'd ever be good enough.

She let out a shaky breath, deciding not to hide from her past this time. "It's my cousin, my family—everything about me."

"You have told me almost nothing about your family. This is the first time I have ever heard you talk about them."

She chewed on her lower lip, still afraid of being judged.

"What about your family, Sabrina? What are you not telling me?"

CHAPTER 10

*S*abrina lowered her eyes. "I didn't have the same childhood you did," she said. "Not even close. No perfect, traditional house with two parents and a loving family. I'm not even sure who my father is. My mother wasn't sure. My father was either her boyfriend or her drug dealer."

Renaldo inhaled sharply.

Sabrina lifted her head. "The reason I never shared my past with you is because it's a past I want to forget. I don't want to remember the things I saw or what I had to do."

Concern etched in his face. "What did you have to do, *meu amor?*"

The gentleness in his voice scraped away the final layer of self-defense. She didn't want to keep everything inside anymore. It was hard being strong all the time. She wanted to unburden her soul. The tears swelled and overflowed onto her cheeks. Sobbing, she fell against the wall and covered her face with her hands.

Renaldo pulled her close. "Shh." He guided her to the sofa and sat down, pulling her onto his lap. In a soothing whisper, he spoke to her in Portuguese.

She told him everything. About how her mother raised her and Jewel in a small, one-bedroom apartment. How she had to go down to the morgue to identify her own mother as a teen. She told him about Jewel's addiction, and how it strained their relationship over the years. In the throes of addiction, Jewel lied to and stole from Sabrina, so Sabrina learned to keep her money, credit cards, or anything else of value locked up or away from her.

She told him about the guilt she continued to feel because maybe if she'd gotten help for her mother, she wouldn't have died. She'd been angry at her mother—even secretly hated her at times. When she passed away, the bottom had fallen out of her world, and she wished she had been less judgmental and more helpful.

"After she died, Jewel and I barely made ends meet," she whispered, hanging her head. "We lied, begged. When we couldn't get what we needed, we stole it—food, clothes—and moved around from place to place, sometimes staying with family, sometimes sleeping wherever we could lay our heads. We did whatever we had to do to survive."

"Couldn't you get help from the state?"

"Yes. But as minors, we didn't want to end up in the foster care system and risk getting split up. We had been through so much together, the thought of getting separated terrified us. When I won a scholarship to go to college, I thought our prayers had been answered. I was able to get additional financial aid, and I wanted to rent a small apartment off campus. That way Jewel could stay with me and finish high school, and if I got a part-time job, we could live more comfortably than we had in years." Sabrina sighed. "But she met an older man and forgot all about school and our plans. They moved in together and everything about her changed after that. He was the worst thing that ever happened to her." Tears clouded her vision. "I wish I could have done something to convince her to leave him."

Renaldo stroked her hair consolingly. "You did the best you could."

She sniffed to keep her nose from running. "What do you think of me now?"

His hand cupped her cheek. "I think what I thought the first time I met you. You are a strong woman. I admire your strength even more now that I know what you've been through. If you thought I would judge you, you're wrong." He smiled ruefully. "You are a better person than I am. Because even after everything that's happened between you and your cousin, you still forgive her. You still protect her."

"She's family. We're all we've got. I won't turn my back on her. She needs love and forgiveness. It's not too late for her, and everyone deserves a second chance."

"You've given her several second chances." He fell silent. "I admire you, Sabrina. I admire your ability to forgive. I have a habit of cutting people off when they hurt me or make a mistake."

"If you love someone, you learn to forgive them," Sabrina said. "Sometimes losing them hurts more than the pain they've caused you. Believe me, when Jewel acts the way she does, I know it's the drugs. When she's herself, she's such a good person—caring and generous to a fault."

"Like you." He traced the fullness of her lips with his thumb.

A tremulous smile graced her lips. "I must look awful right now."

"No, you look beautiful. I missed you these past few days."

"I missed you, too."

He gently kissed each eyelid. "I really, really missed you." His voice sounded husky and filled with longing.

She nodded, emotion clogging her throat.

"I love you, Sabrina." Her gaze flew up to meet his. He cupped her face in his hands. "I couldn't stop thinking about you. I missed talking to you. I missed hearing your voice." He swallowed, brushing a palm over her thick hair. "I thought I was losing my mind. That's why I had to come see you."

"Do you mean it?" It was too good to be true. Not only did he not care about her past, but he loved her, too?

"Yes."

She wrapped her arms around his neck and kissed him hard on the mouth. "I love you, too."

"Do you mean it?" he teased with a smile, echoing her question.

"Yes!" She kissed him again. Her body pressed closer to the hard planes of his, as he cupped her bottom and prolonged the kiss.

Finally, he lifted his head and whispered, "How are you with long distance relationships?"

"I've never been in one, but we can make it work, right? I mean, Brazil is far away, but you'll be back and forth now, won't you?"

He nodded. "When I come back, I want to see you. Every day." He kissed her. "Every night." He kissed her again. "I want to spend every moment I can with you when we're not working."

"I wouldn't want it any other way," Sabrina said. She felt light-headed and drunk with happiness.

"Let's not go out. Let's stay here. I leave tomorrow, and I want to spend as much time alone with you as possible."

Sabrina nodded her agreement. She rose from the sofa. She took Renaldo's hand and led him into her bedroom.

CHAPTER 11

*T*he next morning, Renaldo reluctantly dragged himself from Sabrina's warm bed and soft arms. He dressed in silence and declined the steaming cup of coffee she offered. He had no appetite for drink or food.

At the door, they kissed one last time. He crushed her to him, running his hands up and down her body through the silk robe, trying to imprint her shape in his mind until he could see her again. As if he could forget anything about her. He couldn't. Not her long legs, the flair of her hips, nor the cushiony feel of her backside. Not her soft lips, her wild kinky hair, nor the scent of pink lilies clinging to his clothes.

She represented everything a man could want. Smart and funny. Strong yet vulnerable. Sexy, and she even laughed at his jokes. She was curious about his culture and wanted to learn his language. For the first time in his life, he didn't look forward to returning home.

Once he left, he moved on leaden feet down the hallway, the tightness in his chest expanding the farther he walked from her door. At the elevator, he punched the button and stepped into the open cabin. As the doors closed, he thought back to their conversation. They'd agreed to continue seeing each other when he came back to the States. It seemed like a good idea, but in the bright light of day, he realized it wouldn't be enough.

The elevator stopped and two women entered, smiled at him, and then resumed their conversation with each other.

Worry seeped into his bones as the doors closed. What would she do when he wasn't here? Would she date other men? Would she restart her friendship with her "friend" who had stood her up the night they met?

He thought about his parents' loving relationship, which served as a blueprint for the type of marriage he wanted. In the short time since he'd met Sabrina, he'd felt they could have the same type of relationship.

There was one more characteristic he admired in her. She had a strong work ethic, like he did. With her intelligence and knowledge, she should be making strides at the firm where she worked. Instead, she continued to be overlooked and remained unhappy.

An idea popped into Renaldo's head. It made perfect sense. He pushed the button for the next floor and exited the elevator when it stopped. With a newfound burst of energy, he sprinted up the stairs, back to Sabrina's apartment.

* * *

A LOUD KNOCK on the door startled Sabrina from her moping. She stood at the kitchen counter, staring down into a cup of coffee that had grown cold. Frowning, she went to the door, and for the second time in less than twenty-four hours, she opened it to let Renaldo in.

"Did you forget something?"

"You." He walked in and shut the door.

"What do you mean?" Sabrina asked, her heart rate picking

up speed. She didn't want to jump to conclusions about what he'd just implied, but he looked so intense.

"On the way down in the elevator, I realized I don't want to see you every few months or whenever I can get away and come back. It's not enough. The past few days have taught me that." He cupped her face in his hands, his dark eyes staring intently down into hers. "Marry me. Come to Brazil and become my partner, in my personal life as well as in business. Help me build my company."

Sabrina's mouth fell open. "Marry you?"

He nodded. "Have you been happy over the past month?"

She nodded.

"Are you certain of your feelings for me? Certain you love me?"

She nodded. "Yes."

"Then marry me."

"But my job—"

"You do not need that job. They don't appreciate you. You are an intelligent woman, and I trust your judgment. In the short time I've known you, you have given me good advice that I put to use when I purchased the Samson Hotel. Think about it—as partners we could grow the business and be unstoppable. You handle the finance side, and I will manage the purchase and renovation of the properties. We could do this."

"You're serious?"

"Yes." He smiled down at her. "Say yes, because I won't accept any other answer. *Te amo com todo meu coração.*"

"What does that mean?" Sabrina asked.

"I love you with all my heart."

Sabrina's fingers encircled his wrists. "You know I love you, too, but I have so much baggage. What about Jewel? I can't just abandon her. She needs me."

He paused and thought for a moment. "Then bring her with

you. In my country, family is very important. When we marry, your family becomes mine, and my family becomes yours."

"She has a drug problem," Sabrina reminded him. "It's very difficult to deal with. I can't ask you to become a part of this."

"Do you think there are no treatment facilities in Brazil? She can receive excellent care there, and maybe the change of environment will be good for her."

"I've never been out of the country before, and I don't even speak Portuguese."

"You can learn."

He had an answer for every objection she tossed out. Sabrina blinked, trying to digest his words. "This is happening so fast!" she said with a shaky laugh.

He took her hands in his. "Are you afraid?"

She bit the inside of her lower lip. "A little. What if it doesn't work?"

"It will work. We're compatible in every way."

"We haven't even talked about the basics. What about kids?"

"Yes, I want them."

She laughed. "Me, too, eventually, but not right now."

"Me, either. We'll be too busy working. Maybe in three or four years?"

"Okay...well, how many?"

"Four."

"Four! No way. One."

"One?" He looked aghast. "No. Four."

"Two."

"Okay, three." He grinned.

"Renny! Two. That's my final offer."

"All right." He pulled her into his arms and kissed her temple. His unshaven jaw scraped her skin. "Just say yes. Say you will marry me," he whispered.

She wrapped her arms around his neck. "Yes. I'll marry you."

He growled with joy and swung her around in a circle. Her

joyous laughter filled the room. When he set her back on her feet, she pressed her lips against his.

"We're really doing this?"

"We are really doing this," he confirmed.

His eyes lit up with happiness, but a small part of her hesitated. She couldn't wait to turn in her resignation, and she agreed a change of location might be good for Jewel. Getting her away from the old life and the temptations presented here in Chicago could be what she needed. Life would improve for both of them.

She'd be a partner in a real estate investment company, and as a bonus, she'd be married to a sexy man who adored her. It was perfect. And that's what she feared. It was too perfect.

"Promise me something," she said, looking deeply into his eyes.

"Anything." He continued to smile down at her. Noting her somber expression, he frowned and asked, "What is it?"

"Promise me you'll always love me." He laughed, as if her request was ridiculous. She squeezed his hands in hers. "Promise."

"*Meu amor,*" he said, "you have nothing to fear. My love is real. I know we will be happy together. Believe me, there is nothing you could ever do that would make me stop loving you."

Sabrina stroked his cheek and allowed herself to bask in the warmth of his love. "Good," she said. "Because I can't wait to be your wife."

Check out the entire Latin Men series with heroes from Mexico, Ecuador, Brazil, and Argentina: The Arrangement, Fight for Love, Private Acts, The Ultimate Merger, Second Chances, More Than a Mistress, and Undeniable.

ABOUT THE AUTHOR

Delaney Diamond is the USA Today Bestselling Author of sweet, sensual, passionate romance novels. Originally from the U.S. Virgin Islands, she now lives in Atlanta, Georgia. She reads romance novels, mysteries, thrillers, and a fair amount of nonfiction. When she's not busy reading or writing, she's in the kitchen trying out new recipes, dining at one of her favorite restaurants, or traveling to an interesting locale.

Enjoy free reads on her website. Join her mailing list to get sneak peeks, notices of sale prices, and find out about new releases.

Join her mailing list
www.delaneydiamond.com

 facebook.com/DelaneyDiamond
twitter.com/DelaneyDiamond
bookbub.com/authors/delaney-diamond
pinterest.com/delaneydiamond

www.ingramcontent.com/pod-product-compliance
Lightning Source LLC
Chambersburg PA
CBHW070810120626
46557CB00002B/798